Dear Parent:
Your child's love of reading starts here!

Every child learns to read in a different way and at his or her own speed. Some go back and forth between reading levels and read favorite books again and again. Others read through each level in order. You can help your young reader improve and become more confident by encouraging his or her own interests and abilities. From books your child reads with you to the first books he or she reads alone, there are I Can Read Books for every stage of reading:

SHARED READING
Basic language, word repetition, and whimsical illustrations, ideal for sharing with your emergent reader

BEGINNING READING
Short sentences, familiar words, and simple concepts for children eager to read on their own

READING WITH HELP
Engaging stories, longer sentences, and language play for developing readers

READING ALONE
Complex plots, challenging vocabulary, and high-interest topics for the independent reader

ADVANCED READING
Short paragraphs, chapters, and exciting themes for the perfect bridge to chapter books

I Can Read Books have introduced children to the joy of reading since 1957. Featuring award-winning authors and illustrators and a fabulous cast of beloved characters, I Can Read Books set the standard for beginning readers.

A lifetime of discovery begins with the magical words "I Can Read!"

Visit www.icanread.com for information on enriching your child's reading experience.

For Mimi—a friend
forever
—R.P.G.

For A.B.: my long-sleeve
plaid flannel friend
—T.E.

HarperCollins®, ▣®, and I Can Read Book® are trademarks of HarperCollins Publishers.

Fancy Nancy: Pajama Day Text copyright © 2009 by Jane O'Connor Illustrations copyright © 2009 by Robin Preiss Glasser All rights reserved. Printed in the United States of America. No part of this book may be used or reproduced in any manner whatsoever without written permission except in the case of brief quotations embodied in critical articles and reviews. For information address HarperCollins Children's Books, a division of HarperCollins Publishers, 10 East 53rd Street, New York, NY 10022.
www.icanread.com

Library of Congress Cataloging-in-Publication Data
O'Connor, Jane.
  Pajama Day / by Jane O'Connor ; cover illustration by Robin Preiss Glasser ; interior pencils by Ted Enik ; color by Carolyn Bracken. — 1st ed.
    p. cm. — (Fancy Nancy) (I can read! Level 1)
  Summary: Nancy, who likes to use fancy words, is excited to wear her elegant nightgown for Pajama Day at school, until her best friend, Bree, and Clara impress everyone by wearing matching pink polka-dot pajamas.
  ISBN 978-0-06-189388-9
  [1. Pajamas—Fiction. 2. Friendship—Fiction. 3. Schools—Fiction. 4. Vocabulary—Fiction.] I. Enik, Ted, ill. II. Title.
PZ7.O222Paj 2009   2008027472
[E]—dc22   CIP
                                                                                                                                        AC

09 10 11 12   LP/WOR   10 9 8 7 6 5 4 3 2 1   ❖   First Edition

I Can Read!

BEGINNING
1
READING

Fancy NANCY Pajama Day

by Jane O'Connor

cover illustration by Robin Preiss Glasser

interior pencils by Ted Enik

color by Carolyn Bracken

HarperCollinsPublishers

"Class, don't forget!"

Ms. Glass says.

"Tomorrow is . . ."

"Pajama Day!" we shout in unison.

(That's a fancy word

for all together.)

I plan to wear my new nightgown.
I must say, it is very elegant!
(Elegant is a fancy word
for fancy.)

Then the phone rings.

It is Bree.

She says, "I am going to wear
my pajamas with pink hearts
and polka dots.

Do you want to wear yours?

We can be twins!"

"Ooh!" I say.

"Being twins would be fun."

Then I look at my elegant nightgown.

What a dilemma!

(That's a fancy word for problem.)

Finally I make up my mind.

I tell Bree I am going to wear

my brand-new nightgown.

Bree understands.

She is my best friend.

She knows how much

I love being fancy.

The next morning at school,
we can't stop laughing.
Everyone's in pajamas,
even the principal.
He is carrying a teddy bear.

Ms. Glass has on a long nightshirt
and fuzzy slippers.
I am the only one
in a fancy nightgown.
That makes me unique!
(You say it like this: you-NEEK.)

"Nancy, look!" says Bree.
"Clara has on the same
pajamas as me."

14

Bree and Clara giggle.

"We're twins!" says Clara.

"And we didn't even plan it."

At story hour, Ms. Glass

has us spread out our blankets.

She reads a bedtime story.

Clara and Bree lie
next to each other.
"We're twins,"
Clara keeps saying.

At recess

Clara takes Bree's hand.

They run to the monkey bars.

"Come on, Nancy," Bree calls.

But it is hard to climb in
a long nightgown.
And I can't hang upside down.
Everyone would see
my underpants!

At lunch

I sit with Bree and Clara.

They both have grape rolls

in their lunch boxes.

"Isn't that funny, Nancy?"

asks Clara.

"We even have the same dessert."

I do not reply.

(That's a fancy word for answer.)

Pajama Day is not turning out

to be much fun.

I wanted to be fancy and unique.

Instead I feel excluded.

(That's fancy for left out.)

The afternoon is no better.

Clara and Bree are partners

in folk dancing.

Robert steps on my hem.
Some of the lace trim
on my nightgown rips.

At last the bell rings.

I am glad Pajama Day is over.

"Do you want to come
play at my house?"
I ask Bree.

But Bree can't come.

She's going to Clara's house!

I know it's immature.

(That's fancy for babyish.)

But I almost start to cry.

Then, as we are leaving,

Bree and Clara rush over.

"Nancy, can you come play too?"

Clara asks.

"Yes!" I say.

"I just have to go home first
to change."

Now we are triplets!

Fancy Nancy's Fancy Words

These are the fancy words in this book:

Dilemma—a problem

Elegant—fancy

Excluded—left out

Immature—babyish

Reply—answer

Unique—one of a kind (you say it like this: you-NEEK)

Unison—all together

Fancy Nancy's Fancy Words

These are the fancy words in this book:

Biography—a story about a real person

Crestfallen—sad and ashamed

Dazzling—eye-popping, a knockout

Desperate—feeling trapped

Heroine—a girl or a woman who is brave and helps people

Plume—feather

Select—to pick

Thrilling—even more exciting than exciting

Sacajawea was a heroine.

Ms. Glass is a heroine too.

At least, she is to me!

So I do.

I tell them all about

the brave things Sacajawea did.

Ms. Glass understands.

"Why don't you tell the class
about your book?"

I am crestfallen.

(That is fancy for sad and ashamed.)

"I spent too much time
on the cover,"
I tell Ms. Glass.

I read my report.

"Sacajawea was a heroine.

She helped people in trouble."

Everybody waits to hear more.

But there is no more.

But hearing other reports
makes me nervous.
All of them are longer
than mine.
All of them are more interesting.

The next day,

everyone sees my cover

and says, "Wow!"

Mom lets me stay up longer.
Still my report ends up
only two sentences long.

I have to hand in my report tomorrow!

"I am desperate!" I tell Mom.

(That means I'm in trouble.)

The trouble is, I am tired.

I know all about Sacajawea.

But the right words won't come.

What am I going to do?

Now I will write my report.

I get out lined paper

and a pen with a plume.

(That's a fancy word for feather.)

Ta-da! The cover is finished.

Sacajawea has yarn braids.

Beads and fringe are glued

on her clothes.

I must admit it is dazzling.

(That is fancy for eye-popping.)

"Ms. Glass wants you
to write about the book,"
Dad says over and over.
"That's what a report is."
"I know that!" I tell him.
Writing the words will be easy.

"Just remember to
leave time for the words,"
Mom keeps saying.
"I will. I will," I tell her.

I start working on the cover.

I work on it every night.

I make Sacajawea look very brave,

because she was.

She found food for the explorers.

She kept them safe from enemies.

I get a bag of little beads,

some yarn,

and markers.

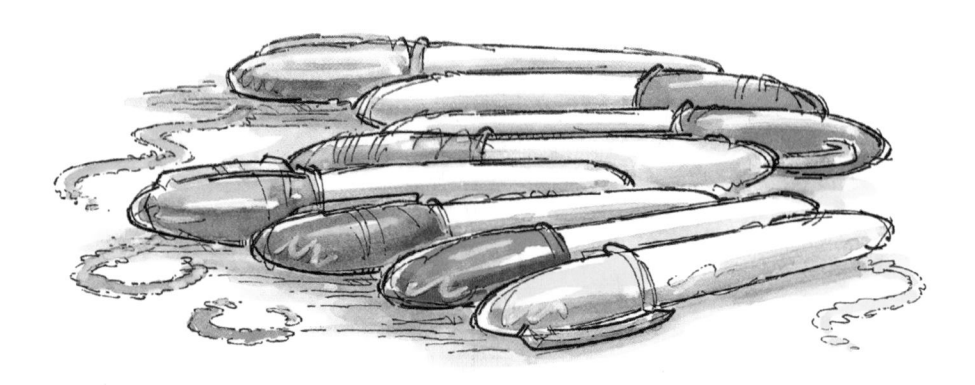

(I am the second-best artist

in our class.

This isn't bragging.

You can ask anybody.)

Mom takes me to the art store.

I need stuff for

the cover of my book report.

I want it to be great!

After dinner I read my book.

Dad helps with the hard words.

I learn all about Sacajawea.

Sacajawea was a princess.

She lived two hundred years ago

out West.

She helped two explorers

reach the Pacific Ocean.

"Yes, I know," I say.

"My book is a biography.

It is about a real person."

"Your first book report.

How grown up!"

my mom says at dinner.

10

Later Ms. Glass has
thrilling news.
(Thrilling is even more exciting
than exciting.)
We get to do a book report!

I select a book

about an Indian girl.

She has a fancy name,

Sacajawea.

You say it like this:

SACK-uh-jah-WAY-ah.

Bree selects a book on dinosaurs.

Robert selects a book
of funny poems.

Teddy selects a scary story.

Before we leave, we select a book.

(Select is a fancy word for pick.)

It is like getting a present

for a week!

Monday is my favorite day.

Why?

Monday is Library Day.

I Can Read!

BEGINNING 1 READING

Fancy NANCY

The Dazzling Book Report

by Jane O'Connor

cover illustration by Robin Preiss Glasser

interior illustrations by Ted Enik

HarperCollins*Publishers*

For Owen Anastas,
a dazzling reader
—J.O'C.

For my dazzling *friend*
Sue Littman
—R.P.G.

For P.S., who saw the
potential joy contained
in a rainbow pack of
construction paper
—T.E.

HarperCollins®, 📚®, and I Can Read Book® are trademarks of HarperCollins Publishers.

Fancy Nancy: The Dazzling Book Report
Text copyright © 2009 by Jane O'Connor
Illustrations copyright © 2009 by Robin Preiss Glasser
All rights reserved. Printed in the United States of America.
No part of this book may be used or reproduced in any manner whatsoever without written permission except in the case of brief quotations embodied in critical articles and reviews. For information address HarperCollins Children's Books, a division of HarperCollins Publishers, 10 E 53rd Street, New York, NY. 10022
www.icanread.com

Library of Congress Cataloging-in-Publication Data
O'Connor, Jane.
The dazzling book report / by Jane O'Connor ; cover illustration by Robin Preiss Glasser ; interior illustrations by Ted Enik. — 1st ed.
    p. cm. — (Fancy Nancy) (I can read! Level 1)
    Summary: Nancy is determined to make the cover of her very first book report as fancy as she can, but she spends so much time on it that she has no time to write about the book.
    ISBN 978-0-06-189388-9
    [1. Homework—Fiction. 2. Schools—Fiction. 3. Vocabulary—Fiction.] I. Preiss-Glasser, Robin, ill. II. Enik, Ted, ill. III. Title.
PZ7.O222Daz 2009   2008024646
[E]—dc22   CIP
                                                                                                                        AC

09 10 11 12 LP/WOR 10 9 8 7 6 5 4 3 2 1

❖

First Edition

Dear Parent:
Your child's love of reading starts here!

Every child learns to read in a different way and at his or her own speed. Some go back and forth between reading levels and read favorite books again and again. Others read through each level in order. You can help your young reader improve and become more confident by encouraging his or her own interests and abilities. From books your child reads with you to the first books he or she reads alone, there are I Can Read Books for every stage of reading:

SHARED READING
Basic language, word repetition, and whimsical illustrations, ideal for sharing with your emergent reader

BEGINNING READING
Short sentences, familiar words, and simple concepts for children eager to read on their own

READING WITH HELP
Engaging stories, longer sentences, and language play for developing readers

READING ALONE
Complex plots, challenging vocabulary, and high-interest topics for the independent reader

ADVANCED READING
Short paragraphs, chapters, and exciting themes for the perfect bridge to chapter books

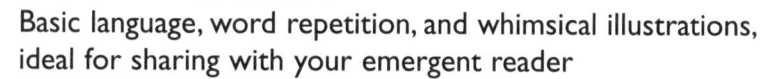

I Can Read Books have introduced children to the joy of reading since 1957. Featuring award-winning authors and illustrators and a fabulous cast of beloved characters, I Can Read Books set the standard for beginning readers.

A lifetime of discovery begins with the magical words "I Can Read!"

Visit www.icanread.com for information
on enriching your child's reading experience.